The
Most
Beautiful
Gift

JONATHAN SNOW

The Most Beautiful Gift

WARNER BOOKS

A Time Warner Company

Warner Books, Inc., 1271 Avenue of the Americas, New York, NY 10020

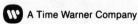 A Time Warner Company

Printed in the United States of America
First Printing: November 1996
10 9 8 7 6 5 4 3 2 1

Library of Congress Cataloging-in-Publication Data

Snow, Jonathan.
    The most beautiful gift / Jonathan Snow.
        p. cm.
    Summary: Enraptured when he sees his first snowflake just before Christmas, Mark, a seven-year-old boy living in Italy, searches for just the right person to give the treasure he has saved.
    ISBN 0-446-52082-9
    1. Christmas stories. [1. Christmas—Fiction. 2. Snow—Fiction. 3. Grandfathers—Fiction.] I. Title.
PR9120.9.S65M6 1996
823'.914[Fic]—dc20   96-16137
                                            CIP
                                            AC

Book design and composition by Giorgetta Bell McRee

To my father, for Pilgrim and the rest

The
Most
Beautiful
Gift

The
Snowflake

Mark was sitting in front of the fireplace. Holding a crayon in his hand, he was trying to color a hopping bunny rabbit in his coloring book. The choice was rather difficult: a beautiful sky blue? "Bunnies don't exist like that," whispered a little voice from somewhere nearby, although it wasn't clear just where. "Not even on Mars?" asked the little boy. Talking to himself made him feel more comfortable, if for nothing else, because it seemed as if someone was always near—perhaps another boy just like him. At eight years old, you can never have enough friends.

"No, not even on Mars!" His invisible companion did not want to concede.

Mark raised his can of Dr. Pepper and examined its bright red metallic color. That might be the right color. Before the little voice could protest, Mark pressed his crayon several times across the figure of the bunny. After a few minutes, the animal was transformed into a big, fat, ripe cherry.

"Not bad," said the boy, studying the drawing in the dim light of December. "Not bad at all." Now he had to choose the color for the rest of the picture: for the pine tree with its big big eyes; for the badger wearing a mountain cap; for the stars that twinkled high in the sky and almost seemed to smile.

Looking for inspiration, Mark turned his gaze toward the window. The sky was gray and the air seemed to stand still. Here and there, what looked like dandelion seeds floated by. But they weren't seeds. Spring was still a long time away. Christmas was already knocking at the door. There were only two days to go.

"Snow!" yelled Mark, pushing aside his coloring book. He narrowly avoided spilling his can of Dr. Pepper. If he had, the mess would have caused his mom and dad to change into two crazy people, yelling and screaming, deafening him with their scolding.

Mark quickly put on a pair of boots, grabbed his coat, and hurried outside. The snowflakes fell over Spring Valley like tiny cotton puffs, like small tufts of the sweetest cotton candy. There weren't many flakes. The snowfall was little more than a dusting of cinnamon over an apple pie, but the boy didn't seem to mind. It was the first sign of Christmas. Who knew whether his parents, shut up in their offices in the city, were also enjoying the show? No, they were probably bent over their work, over page after page to read, approve, sign. They would come home in the evening with weary expressions and the worn-out look of people who rushed around all day doing things they would gladly have avoided.

Mark craned his neck skyward to discover where the snow was coming from. Surely somebody had to be scattering it. Maybe there was a Snowman, just as there was a Sandman who came very quietly at night to put you to sleep by sprinkling your eyes with magic dust. But no matter how far he stretched, Mark wasn't able to see anything. Perhaps the mysterious little man was hiding among the clouds with his snowmaking machine—a kind of enormous ice grater churning out the world's largest Italian ices! It was probably up there somewhere, hidden from prying eyes.

A snowflake landed on Mark's nose. The boy stared down at it intently. It was beautiful. It looked like a minuscule glass star, made by the most talented artist in the world; or a diamond, discovered deep down in the earth and brought up into the open air for the very first time, finally free, and expressing its joy with vibrant rays of light.

Mark took the snowflake between two fingers, careful not to melt it, and placed it in the palm of his hand. The tiny crystal flake almost hypnotized him with its iridescent colors. With extreme care, as if he was holding in his hands a priceless treasure, he headed for home. He opened the door and aimed for the kitchen. Everything was immersed in a silence that only snow can bring. From the next room drifted the snores of Grampa Gus, who was taking his usual afternoon nap. Around five o'clock in the afternoon, he would wake up, prepare himself a cup of hot milk, and then he would entertain his grandson with one of his stories about pirates and sailors, princes and princesses, aliens from outer space and giants from unknown lands. Mark loved to listen to his tales and could never hear enough of them.

The boy opened the refrigerator and peered at the contents inside: a carton of milk, a container of Sunkist orange juice, a stack of ready-made meals in their silver packaging. Those precooked dishes were his parents' only diet, but Mark longed for something different. To tell the truth, every so often even his mother and father seemed to eat them reluctantly, even though they didn't want to prepare something else.

"Why feed yourself that junk?" asked the same little voice. "It's much better to munch on a green apple, or on a sweet, juicy pear, than to stuff yourself with that tasteless garbage."

Mark put aside his thoughts of food as he reached into the refrigerator; today, it would serve a more important purpose. No, it wasn't cold enough. The snowflake might melt. In fact, it was already changing into water right there on his finger. Worried, he opened the freezer. A large turkey welcomed him. The turkey was probably also precooked, and had a little dish of cranberry sauce covered in cellophane by its side. His parents were consistent. The enormous beast, the size of a baby dinosaur, occupied all of the available space except for a tiny corner next to the ice tray. Better than nothing, Mark thought. With extreme care, he put his snow crystal there and closed the door. "What are you doing?" demanded the little voice. "Have you gone crazy? Why do you want to keep a snowflake?"

The boy didn't even bother to respond. In his heart he had already come up with a plan: He would give the snowflake to the best person in the world. It would be a magnificent gift—his crystal was the most beautiful of all, different from all the others. As his teacher once said, there are no two snowflakes exactly alike. And this one was simply stupendous. He glanced at the clock hanging on the wall in the kitchen— ten minutes to four. He would have to find the best person in the universe before his parents got home. Otherwise, his plan was sure to fail. He could already hear their comments: "Give a snowflake as a gift? How silly! And to whom?" Furthermore, they surely wouldn't have let him go out by himself. He turned his gaze toward the window. It had already stopped snowing, which meant his gift would be even more valuable. No one else would be able to give or receive one like it.

Mark headed to the front door and slowly opened it. From Grampa Gus's room came the usual soft snores; the old man didn't stir. That's lucky, thought the boy as he went outside in search of the person who would deserve his treasured gift.

Jack's
General
Store

When Mark entered the store, Jack Skelly was busy stacking a shelf with canned corn. Jack was a robust man with perennially rosy cheeks and a sprinkling of gray in his hair. Mark liked him. Often he would give Mark licorice sticks, or caramels, or candied fruit. However, despite the affection Mark felt toward him, he needed to make sure that Mr. Skelly truly deserved his gift.

"Hello, Mr. Skelly," Mark greeted him as he neared.

"Oh, hello, Mark," he replied. "What an unexpected treat! Shouldn't you be in school?"

"School is out. We're all on vacation. There are only two days left until Christmas."

The man shook his head. "Wow, you're right. Even though I've hung ornaments and wreaths in the window, I keep forgetting." He placed one more can of Green Giant corn at the very top of the stack, then rubbed his hands together, satisfied. "Well, Mark, can I do something for you?"

The boy was silent for a moment. He didn't know what to say. Then all of a sudden, an idea flashed through his mind. "Yes, Mr. Skelly," he said resolutely. "For a homework assignment during vacation, our teacher asked us to do some research."

"Research?" asked Jack, curious. "What kind of research?"

"Well, she wants us to ask different people a specific question, and then write the answers in a notebook." Mark was fully aware he was telling a lie, but, after all, it was just a white lie. In other words, he was lying, but he wasn't hurting anyone. As Grampa Gus often said, white lies help

14

you to help others, to hide a truth better left unrevealed. After all, white lies help you ward off the black lies, the worst lies—the ones that are so bad, they parch your throat when you say them.

Jack smiled and scratched his head. "Well, if I can be of any help, I'm glad to oblige." He chuckled. "Even if I'm only a poor merchant and not a rocket scientist."

The boy laughed in turn. "The question is very easy. If someone gave you a snowflake, what would you do with it?"

Mr. Skelly remained perplexed for a moment. "A snowflake?" he finally asked.

"Yes."

He scratched his head once again. "It would be a rather strange gift. But let me think. . . ." A few minutes passed, then he said, "Well, I believe I would put it inside a tin can with a beautiful label."

Mark thought he had misunderstood. Or maybe he just didn't want to believe his ears. "You mean you would . . . you would sell it?"

"Of course!" replied the man, with glee. "Otherwise, I would have no idea what to do with it. But some of my customers might appreciate it. If I was successful in selling the first can, I would make many more. During a snowfall, I would collect a whole pile of snowflakes, put them in cans, and continue to sell them. Not a bad idea at all. I can already picture the writing on the label: JACK SKELLY'S GENUINE SNOWFLAKES! NO ARTIFICIAL COLORING OR PRESERVATIVES! STORE IN A COOL PLACE! BEWARE OF IMITATIONS!"

Mark was overcome by the desire to get out of the store. He came up with an excuse for why he had to go, and he left Mr. Skelly to his cans of corn. Walking down Spring Valley's main street, he brooded, muttering to himself. Or maybe he was talking to the little voice—he could no longer be sure. "Put a snowflake in a can? How could someone even think of such nonsense? It would be like putting a robin in a cage, or trying to catch a rainbow, or stealing the pure mountain air and putting it in a spray can! Snow is beautiful because it flies free in the sky, carried along by air currents. The person who deserves my snowflake must understand these things."

Dr. Lands

A thin, bald man with thick eyeglasses greeted Mark with a strong handshake. "Well, my friend, I hope you haven't come because of anything serious. Even if it's only a bump on your behind, for example. Something so simple can still be a big pain!" And he laughed heartily.

Mark looked around him. The wall was decorated with a picture of a skeleton and a NO SMOKING sign. The office was empty. Dr. Lands scheduled almost all of his appointments in the morning, and during the afternoon only a few patients stopped in.

"No thanks, I feel great. I only wanted to ask you a question. . . ." Mark told him about his assignment, trying his hardest to be convincing. This time, he was talking to a doctor, not a simpleton like Mr. Skelly. He sincerely hoped that the doctor's response would be the right one.

The doctor let Mark finish his explanation, cleaned his glasses with a corner of his lab coat, then said, "It seems to me to be a very interesting question." His bald head shone with the brightness of a lamp; perhaps it lighted up like that when he got an idea. "The first thing I would do is put the snowflake on a glass slide and study it under the microscope."

"But it would melt!" Mark objected. Already things hadn't gotten off to the best start, but the remainder of the conversation looked as if it was only going to get worse.

"No, no, no," said Dr. Lands, shaking his head. "Nothing of the sort would happen, because I would use a fixing solution made of . . ." He threw up his hands. "Well, you wouldn't understand. Let's just say it's a kind of glue that would keep it from dissolving into water. Or I could use liquid nitrogen. I would then be able to study the crystal structures. They are stupendous, you know, when you look at them through a microscope."

"But a snowflake is beautiful even to the naked eye," insisted the boy, disappointed for a second time.

"Science sees very badly with the naked eye," responded the doctor, tapping his finger against his eyeglasses in order to emphasize the truth of what he was saying.

Mark resisted the temptation to cover his ears with the palms of his hands. In the name of science, the doctor wanted to destroy the most perfect creation he had ever seen.

"Nature," suggested the little voice, "is something beautiful that we must do our best to protect, or else we will lose it forever."

"I would definitely use an electronic microscope," continued Dr. Lands. The boy didn't want to stay to hear any more. He didn't have the strength. He went away discouraged, with his head lowered. From the wall, the skeleton seemed to be sneering maliciously at him, almost as if he were making fun of Mark's sadness.

Louis,
the
Philosopher

Louis Lords lived in a small house not far from Spring Valley's main street. For a couple of years, he had taught philosophy in a college in a nearby city. He then got tired of it and retreated to a private life, together with his half a dozen cats.

When Mark knocked on the door of Mr. Lords's house, he felt a shiver go up his spine. According to his mother, Mr. Lords was a strange man and it was better to stay away from him. But maybe, precisely for this reason, he would be the right person to receive the gift of the snowflake.

The door opened and on the threshold appeared a lanky, longhaired man with an earring and a checkered shirt covered with stains. The boy was tempted to run away as fast as his feet would carry him. "Be brave. Have courage!" he told himself, then repeated to Mr. Lords the same story about the school assignment. When he had finished his explanation, Mr. Lords indicated to the boy with a slight nod of his head that he should come inside.

The house consisted of one enormous room, which functioned as living room, kitchen, and bedroom. Cats were everywhere: lying on the sofa, on top of the refrigerator, even in the sink. Mr. Lords sat down on an old couch the color of green mold and Mark did the same.

"A snowflake," said the man with deliberate slowness. Behind him was a bookshelf overflowing with books. The titles were nearly incomprehensible: *The Critique of Pure Reason, Either/Or, Anti Oedipus.* Only a philosopher would have understood them. Perhaps Mark had really found the right guy.

"It's a strange assignment," Mr. Lords continued, lighting a cigarette with an odd aromatic and penetrating odor.

"It's my teacher's fault," replied the child.

"Right." Louis inhaled deeply a couple of times and caressed an ash-colored cat who had curled up in his lap. "Teachers have no idea what to do anymore." He let out a long sigh. "So, we were talking about a snowflake."

"Exactly." Mark pinched his nose between his thumb and forefinger. The cat hair mixed with the smoke was making him want to sneeze.

"Do you intend the snowflake to be the signifier or the signified?"

"I . . ." The boy didn't know how to respond. Actually, to tell the truth, he didn't understand a word of what Mr. Lords was saying.

"Essentially, it's a hermeneutical problem," continued the philosopher, unaware of his young guest's state of confusion. "Perhaps even eschatological: Where does snow originate and where will it end?" With three long puffs, he finished the cigarette and tossed in onto the stone floor, stamping it out with the heel of his shoe. The area around it was covered with butts.

"From the sky. It comes down from the sky and falls on the earth," Mark answered. All those big words were bothering him.

Louis Lords shook his head. He closed his eyes halfway, as if he was meditating, and brought a finger to his lips. "This is only how it appears. In reality, everything has a primal birth and an ultimate end. If we consider snow . . ."

Mark's head was beginning to spin. It may also have been due to the cat hair and the smoke. In any case, he realized that with Louis Lords, he was going nowhere fast. He got up from the couch and tiptoed toward the door while the man continued his ravings. "If the Greek word *éscate* means the end—or rather, the fall—I wonder which principle, seeing as this also concerns a kind of fall, would be applied to ice crystals. Now taking into careful consideration . . ."

Mark slipped away, closing the door behind

him. Outside, Mr. Lords's words continued to echo. "Utter nonsense," the little voice pointed out to Mark. "In the time it would take this hack philosopher to make a decision, your snowflake would be good and melted." Mark nodded and glanced at his watch. Half past five. His parents would be home soon from the office. And he hadn't solved a thing.

Grampa
Gus

On his way home, Mark met up with other people. He asked all of them the same question, with the same result: zilch. According to Jenny, a classmate of his who was always impeccably dressed, "The snowflake would be very happy in my dollhouse." Harry, a playmate who adored the Power Rangers cartoon characters, told him that he would transform the snowflake into a mutant robot. How exactly, he didn't know, but he would find a way. The owner of Spring Valley's newsstand, Mr. Peabody, even suggested selling the snowflake as part of the Sunday paper supplement.

When he opened the door to his house, Mark wasn't able to hide his bad mood. He kicked the doormat while impatiently unbuttoning his coat: "Is it possible that no one can give me the right answer? Everyone only thinks about selling the snowflake, or studying it, as if it were a circus animal. How disgusting!" He shuffled to the kitchen, where Grampa Gus was having his usual snack. It was kind of fascinating to watch the old man dunk his cookie into his glass of milk, pull it out, and then cram it in his mouth. For some reason, that series of gestures soothed Mark, lightening his very black mood—at least somewhat.

"Grandson, you went out without telling me. You know very well that your parents would not be at all happy about that." Grampa Gus had a large wave of white hair that fell over his forehead and resembled sea foam on a stormy day. His eyes were sky blue and the wrinkles around them only accentuated their brightness. His mouth was always relaxed in a calm and reassuring smile. It was impossible not to love him. He was the sweetest person on earth. He had come to live with them after his wife died, several years ago. He didn't seem to suffer from her death anymore. "After all, life is also made up of departures," he loved to repeat.

"Sorry, Grampa. I went out for a walk," Mark replied. "I was hoping it would snow. The day after tomorrow is Christmas, and a Christmas with snow is much more beautiful."

"Well," responded Grampa, nibbling contentedly on a cookie, "at least there was a flurry." He pointed to the street in front of the house; it was just barely dusted white. "You do know, of course, who makes the snow fall?"

Mark took a minute to answer. He was afraid of having to listen again to Louis Lords's weird theories. But this was his grandfather, not some fly-by-night philosopher. So he gathered his courage, stared at the old man, and said in a thin voice, "No, I don't know."

"It's a long story," said Grampa Gus. "Do you have the time and the desire to hear it?"

The boy shot a glance at the refrigerator. The

snowflake would have to stay in there until the next day, or at least until he had found someone to give it to. By now, it was too late to continue his search. He nodded and Grampa smiled.

The Story
of the Angel
Camolino

Well, once upon a time . . . a long, long time ago," Grampa Gus began, "the good Lord decided to organize a competition in paradise. By now, He had already created almost everything: the mountains and the valleys, the oceans and the seas, daytime and nighttime, the moon and the stars, the four seasons, animals in the most bizarre shapes, and even humankind. He was, however, convinced that something was missing. So, one beautiful day he gathered the angels around Him and said, 'Each one of you is to think of an idea. A stupendous idea, mind you. The most competent inventor will be awarded with a halo brighter than everyone else's. You have two earth days' time.'

"Now, it's not that angels are particularly vain, but you must know that they are very attached to their halos: They polish them every day with cloud puffs so that they will shine as brightly as the midday sun. God's challenge was accepted with extreme enthusiasm and the celestial beings went straight to work. For two days, paradise echoed with their loud exclamations, their shouts of joy, and their expressions of defeat.

"When the two earth days had passed, the entire array of angels came before God. They were all in a line, one behind the other, with their wings beating nervously and their halos whirling continuously around their heads, like records on turntables.

"'The first may come forward,' said God, with His powerful voice.

"'Here I am, Lord,' replied the angel, bowing. 'I thought of this: Why don't we have many little flames rain down from the sky regularly so that humankind can keep warm or cook food?'

"The Lord thought about the idea for a moment before a vexed expression shrouded His face. 'Yes, it would be a way for the creatures to warm themselves, but entire forests and buildings would be given over to flames. It doesn't strike me as a great idea, Lucifer. The next may came forward.' And with a wave of His hand, He dismissed him. He did not like Lucifer very much; sometimes he got the strangest ideas in his head. He would have to check up on him more often, before he got into trouble.

"'My Lord,' began the second angel, 'I thought that trees could be created, providing humankind with all their daily needs—from bread, to meat, to clothes with which to cover themselves.'

"God shook His head. 'Such a thing would mean that human beings would no longer have to work in order to obtain what they desired, and they would dedicate themselves to a life of idleness. No, this lovely thought is also a reject.'

"The third angel approached, frightened and

trembling. 'Lord of creation, my idea is to light up the night sky with Your resplendent image so that everyone will acknowledge Your presence in the heavens.'

"God thought a few seconds, then lowered His head in disappointment. 'No, we'll do nothing of the kind. If daytime is fit for work and the thousands of human activities, nighttime is made for sleeping. Furthermore, if I revealed myself so plainly, mankind would be sure of my presence and the concept of faith would no longer exist.'

"Gabriel, the fourth angel, came forward boldly. 'I would create a gigantic typhoon, an enormous blast of air that would clear off the earth every thousand years. By the end of this time period, a civilization has already given all that it has to give, and risks deterioration.'

"God had to shake His head for the umpteenth time. 'In this way, we would take from human beings their power of choice. And furthermore, Gabriel, why do you want to destroy my most successful creation every thousand years? For humans, I know that is a long period of time, but for us it hardly constitutes a bat of the eye. No, this solution doesn't convince me, either.'

"Raphael slowly came forward. 'I was thinking of a new animal. . . . '

"God stared at him. 'Of which one? It seems to me I have already created far too many. Yours would have to be a truly great invention.'

"'My animal would be called a "bumasaur."'

"'Already I don't like the name,' the Lord declared. 'But let's continue. What would he do, your buma—'

"'Bumasaur.'

"'Yes, in brief, this animal you're talking about.'

"'Ah, he would do absolutely nothing. And he wouldn't be useful for anything.'

"'What?' cried God, His patience visibly tried.

"Raphael took a step backward, frightened by God's anger. 'All the animals You have created have some use—for example, the sheep is useful for its wool, the ox for its quality meats, the cow for its milk, the chicken for its eggs, and so on. The bumasaur, on the other hand, wouldn't be useful for absolutely anything: His fleece would be too bristly to be made into cloth, his meat would be inedible, and his character contrary and disobedient. He would do nothing other than take naps and complain the whole day long.'

"'And of what possible use would such an animal be?' the Lord inquired.

"'Absolutely none, as I have said. Humankind would be shown that not everything—or all animals, in this case—has to have a precise purpose.'

"God banged His hands hard against His knees and thunder echoed throughout the heavens. 'Enough! I have listened long enough to your great discoveries!' He snorted derisively. 'If the rest of you have come up with similar ideas, you would be better off keeping them from me.'

"In a split second, almost all the angels moved away, declaring a thousand excuses: Clouds had to be fluffed; halos had to be shined; manna had to be collected. . . . After a few minutes, only one very tiny angel remained. He was wearing a slightly crooked halo, a patched tunic, and a shy expression. His name was Camolino. He was one of the younger angels, and his wings were still short and he had a child's spirit. Often, God had surprised him while he was chasing clouds, or riding piggy-back on lightning bolts, or wandering aimlessly about down on earth, his big eyes widened by the marvels of creation.

"'So, Camolino,' said the Lord. 'I am ready to hear your idea.'

"The angel looked around him. Blushing deeply, he began to stutter: 'W-w-w-well, I—I—I—'

"'Come on, have a little courage,' God prod-ded him. 'Today I heard so much poppycock, a little more won't make any difference.'

"Camolino filled his lungs with air, sniffed, and, all in one breath, began to speak. 'Well, I was thinking about rain. . . .'

"'I already created that more than a month ago! Old news!' the Lord exclaimed.

"'Y-y-yes, I know. But I was thinking that the rain might also be solid. . . .'

"'Solid? What are you prattling on about?'

"The little angel thrust his hand inside his tunic and pulled out a silver goblet. 'If rain gets cold, t-t-this might happen.' While he spoke, he turned the goblet upside down. Out came hundreds of white flakes, light as cotton, and they began to flutter above the clouds.

"Intrigued, God took one in His hand. It melted instantly, turning into water. 'And of what use is your invention?' The tone of His voice was less impatient; it even sounded interested.

"Camolino detected God's change of heart and smiled happily. 'For example, during the winter these white flakes would fall on earth, form a blanket against the frost, and protect the plants. People could also collect the flakes and quench their thirst. When the flakes melted, they could feed the rivers and streams, not to mention all the rest.'

"'Which is? Go on. Go on.' The Lord now appeared to be hanging on Camolino's every word. Ironically, their roles had reversed.

"'This white quilt would soften all sounds, creating a magical atmosphere, almost like in a fairy tale. Children could use it to play with. And, if it fell in December—'

"'And why exactly during that month?' interrupted God.

"The angel lowered his gaze. 'Well, You know, Lord, here news travels fast. If You have chosen December as the month in which Your son will be born on earth, as word has it, this invention of mine would be the most effective way of reminding humanity of the event until the end of time.'

"God stroked His long beard. Besides the gossip, which, by the way, happened to be true, Camolino's idea really pleased Him. 'Yes, it is not a bad idea. These . . . flakes of yours wouldn't be difficult to manufacture, would they? I don't want to waste any time, like I did when I put the salt in the oceans and seas.'

"Camolino shook his head. 'It's all very simple. All you have to do is make the rain very cold and it's a done deal.'

"God seemed truly happy. 'Have you already thought of what to baptize this invention of yours?' He asked.

"'Oh yes.' The angel lowered his head once again and regained the blush of a few minutes earlier. 'I would like to call it snow.'

"'Snow?' And what, dash it, does that mean?'

"'Absolutely nothing,' replied Camolino. 'But it is a short name, easily remembered. And when you repeat it—*sn-ow*—it has all the flavor of winter.'

"God rolled the word around on His tongue for a while without finding anything to complain about. 'Well, if you say so,' He concluded. 'So, snow it is.' He reached out a hand and rested it on the angel's right wing. 'You deserve the prize I promised: a beautiful halo, the brightest of all.'

"The angel bowed his head. 'If You don't mind, Lord, I would prefer something else.'

"'*What?*' burst out God. 'You refuse my gift?'

"'N-n-no.' Camolino started stuttering again. 'I absolutely didn't mean to show a lack

48

of respect. As You know, I am shy, and I would be embarrassed to be seen around with my halo dazzling like a blazing ember. Instead—'

"'Instead?'

"'Instead, I would like to be the one who decides how and when the snow will fall. After all, it wouldn't be an overly important duty, and considering the invention is mine . . .'

"God thought about it for a minute. 'All right,' He finally agreed. 'From now on, you will be the angel responsible for the white flakes. Does this please you?'

"Camolino displayed the appropriate joy with an enormous smile. With a bow, he took his leave from God, lay down on his favorite cloud, and gazed at the panorama below. It was still early July and the sun shone high above the humans' world. The angel couldn't wait until December arrived. In the meantime, he decided to take a nap. His sleep was filled with visions of bright white flakes, cold as ice and light as feathers."

Mom and Dad Return Home

Grampa Gus finished his story together with the last cookie. He looked at Mark, then smiled and winked. "So, do you understand who created snow?"

"Of course," responded the boy, who had drunk in the old man's words as if they were a cup of sweet hot chocolate. "But there is something that isn't clear to me."

Grampa looked at him with surprise. "Go on. What is it?"

"If what Camolino had in mind was to make

the snow fall in December, why is nothing happening right now? And why does it sometimes snow before, or after, the specified period?"

Grampa smoothed his white hair with his hand. "It's very simple. Camolino is a very good angel, maybe even the best of all, but he is very distracted. Often he doesn't count the months very well. As you know, time in heaven does not coincide with human time. On other occasions, he forgets his duty, or gets carried away, and this is how avalanches, snowslides, and other natural disasters originate. Mind you, the little angel doesn't do all this out of nastiness, but out of carelessness."

"A little like when I forget to do my homework," suggested Mark.

Grampa Gus laughed aloud. The sound rang out clear as a crystal and filled anyone who heard it with joy. "Something like that. Although in this particular case, I believe your forgetfulness is premeditated."

The boy knit his brow. "What does 'premeditated' mean?"

"Someone, my dear, who forgets to do their

homework on purpose," the old man responded playfully. "Anyway—"

Grampa was suddenly interrupted by the sound of the door opening. Mark's parents were returning home from work.

"So, aren't you happy to see us?" asked Robert, Mark's father, as he placed his leather briefcase on a kitchen chair. He was a short man, fortyish, with a nice plump face. Somehow, he reminded Mark of one of those marzipan cakes that were sold at bakeries around Christmas.

Mark threw his arms around his father's neck. "I am really happy! Grampa was telling me the story of Camolino."

"The story of whom?" asked his mom, taking off her raincoat. Her blond hair glistened like gold in the kitchen's dim light. Her eyes, made up with mascara, were marked by a few wrinkles.

"A little secret between me and Mark, Judith," Grampa replied.

"Oh, two conspirators!" exclaimed Mark's father, pretending to pull a punch on him. The boy began to laugh. He was happy when they were all together—Grampa, his parents, and himself. When he imagined the perfect family, he remembered those moments.

At the table during dinner, Mark asked his mom and dad the same question he had asked repeatedly all that afternoon. Grampa had already gone to bed with his cup of herb tea and a thriller by one of his favorite authors.

His father responded first. "Oh, I wouldn't know," he said with his mouth full. He jabbed his fork into a chicken breast—precooked, of course. "I would probably stare at the snowflake, waiting for it to melt."

"That's all?" Mark asked, as surprised as ever. Before him was a defrosted ear of corn waiting to be munched on.

"What else should I do? I could hardly save it forever. And besides, the snow puts on a beautiful show when it descends from the sky, not when it falls on the ground."

"It immediately turns to slush," explained

his mother. "You should have seen the city today. Perhaps only a couple of snowflakes fell, and already everything was covered with a layer of filth." She shrugged her shoulders as if to chase away the thought.

Mark sunk his teeth into the ear of corn. The kernels were mushy, swollen with water, and tasteless. If it was up to him, he would grow his own corn and eat it only in the summer. He had to admit, though, that his father did have a flawless argument. When snow falls on the ground, it is almost . . . dead. Who knows whether the little angel Camolino had ever considered such a possibility? In any case, Mark would continue his search the following day. He wouldn't, he couldn't, give up.

After dinner, he diligently helped his mom and dad clear the table, then went straight to bed. *Star Trek,* his favorite TV show, was on, but his thoughts were on other things: the snowflake . . . the snowflake . . . the snowflake.

The

Snowflake

Disappears!

Mark got out of bed at about eight o'clock—too early, considering he was on vacation. He had had a strange dream: There was an angel with short wings and a slightly crooked halo holding a crystal sphere. Inside the ball was a miniature reproduction of Spring Valley. The angel turned it upside down, and snow began to fall in great quantities, covering lawns and rooftops and chimneys. Grampa's story must have affected him more than he had imagined.

The boy headed for the kitchen. His parents

had left a bowl of Cheerios, a jug of milk, and a note: "We'll be home at four." Earlier than usual, Mark thought. On the other hand, it was Christmas Eve, and offices closed early. Sitting in front of the window, Grampa Gus was examining the horizon. In his hands, he held his thriller. As he became aware of his grandson's presence, he whirled around. "Hey, Mark, did you sleep well?"

The boy rubbed his eyes with the back of his hand, then poured the milk into his cereal bowl. "Well enough. I dreamed about an angel."

The old man smiled. "That's absolutely natural. After all, today is December twenty-fourth, even if the snow doesn't want to fall." He sighed a long sigh. "I don't know what I would give to see a white flake. I think I would stare at it as if it were the most precious thing on earth. In fact, Christmas without snow isn't a real Christmas. Let's hope that Camolino remembers to fulfill his duty."

Mark's eyes nearly popped out of their sockets. He swallowed his milk the wrong way. He coughed for several seconds, then said, "What did you say you would do with the snowflake?"

Grampa Gus lifted his eyes toward the sky. "I just told you: I would stare at it as if it were the most precious thing in my possession. Then I think I would throw it up high, so that it might be carried by the wind all the way to heaven, where it would remind Camolino that it was time to roll up the sleeves of his tunic."

The little boy didn't make him repeat it a second time. In one leap, he was at the refrigerator. He opened the freezer door, looked inside, and . . . the turkey was still in its place, still gigantic, and the cranberry sauce gleamed nearby, showing off its bright red color. But the snowflake had disappeared. Actually, to tell the truth, there was only a trace of it left, a minuscule point on top of an ice cube.

"Grampa!" Mark yelled. "My snowflake!"

The old man got up from his seat and went over to the refrigerator. The boy was nearly in tears. "What happened?" asked Grampa Gus. "Did you lose something?"

"Yesterday, I caught a snowflake," Mark said between sobs. "Then I put it inside here so that it wouldn't melt. But now . . . " He pointed to the ice cube with the pimple on top.

Grampa shook his head and began to pat his grandson. "How did such an idea get into your head?"

"I wanted to give it to the best person on earth," continued Mark breathlessly. "So I went around asking everybody what they would do with a snowflake. But their answers were completely wrong." A tear streamed down his cheek. "And this morning, without my even asking, you told me the most beautiful thing I have ever heard."

The old man hugged his grandson. "Didn't you know that the snowflake would become a chip of ice? Snow is, of course, only water."

"N-no," stuttered the little boy.

"Oh well." Grampa shook his head. "This whole thing makes me think of an old story. I think you'd better listen to it."

Mark closed the freezer door, wiped his eyes,

and sat down at the kitchen table. His eyes still burned, but the tears had stopped falling. Grampa sat down in front of him. His white hair was a freshly laundered cloud.

The Story
of the Wizard
Buffello

Once upon a time, in the age of princesses and dragons, there was a very skilled wizard named Buffello.

"Well, this wizard of ours had invented everything there was to invent: the philosopher's stone, which could transform lead into gold; the elixir of life—thanks to which, one could live three hundred or so years; Medusa's eye, which turned flesh into stone; and a hundred love potions, a thousand remedies for gout and toothaches, as well as many other marvels.

His fame extended from one end of the known earth to the other.

"One day, he was summoned before the king. The wizard hurried to the palace, where the sovereign asked him to devise a miraculous invention: the spirit of Christmas. 'During this season, everyone is a much better person,' began the king. 'The people love one another. Evil and malice do not exist. I want you to come up with a potion that will make Christmas last three hundred and sixty-five days a year.'

"Buffello bowed to the king, returned to his laboratory, and went straight to work. He consulted his volumes on both white and black magic, but he soon realized they weren't going to be of any help. He then began to collect herbs and other ingredients: an early fig plucked from the plant during a full moon; a mandrake root yanked from the earth on a Friday with an even-numbered date; bullfrog saliva; albino snail slime; and many other wizardly things. He threw everything into a cauldron, left it to boil for almost an entire day, and then tried out the result on himself. The first time he tasted the mixture, he turned into a pea green bat; the second time, into a Bengali tiger; the third time, into a yellow dwarf with a huge hunchback. He struggled to come up with an antidote as quickly as possible in order to return to his old self, and after several attempts, he succeeded.

"Despite his failure, he refused to give up. He prepared another thousand potions, another hundred elixirs, but none of these produced the desired effect. On one occasion, he succeeded in ridding himself of all the calluses on his right foot—a bit of good luck, but not exactly what the king had ordered. One day, when he was feeling more desperate than usual, and was immersed in multicolored smoke and sparkling fire bursts, his grandson, Buffetto, paid him a visit. He was just a little boy, but he had a firm head on his shoulders and a tongue that could talk a mile a minute.

"'Grampa, what are you making?' asked his grandson, peering into an incessantly boiling cauldron.

"'Leave me alone, Buffetto,' replied the wizard as he added an azure dust to the contents of one of his test tubes. 'If I don't succeed in this project, the king will get very angry. He might even relieve me of my duties as court sorcerer.'

"Buffetto took a look around him. He had never seen a laboratory in such disorder. 'C'mon, Grampa,' he urged. 'What did our sovereign want you to do?'

"'He wanted me to create the spirit of Christmas,' replied Buffello impatiently, 'so that all the people will be good the whole year long, not just one day a year.'

"Buffetto stared at his grandfather and burst out laughing. 'Oh, but that is impossible!'

"'What do you mean, impossible?' demanded the wizard, while emptying the contents of a still into a pot. 'For me, nothing is impossible!'

"The boy continued to laugh, then regained his breath. 'Sure it is! It is an absurd undertaking!'

"Buffello sat down, utterly discouraged. Maybe his grandson had a point. He had dedicated many days to his invention but—aside from curing his calluses—nothing good had come of it.

"'What can I do, then?' he asked in desperation. 'I can't go back to the king empty-handed! He would chase me away! He might even send me into exile!'

"Buffetto looked around him and thought about it for a few seconds. 'There might be a way.' He scratched his chin with the tip of his finger. 'Now then . . .'

"The next day, the wizard presented himself at the palace. He was carrying a large sack. 'Welcome back, Buffello,' the sovereign greeted him. 'So, did you succeed in finding the spirit of Christmas?'

"'Yes, my sire, I have it right inside here,' replied the wizard.

"'Good, well, what are you waiting for?'

"Buffello nodded, clutched the sack with both hands, turned it upside down and out came . . . nothing! Absolutely nothing, not even a magic herb, an enchanted animal, or a chip off the philosopher's stone.

"'And what does this mean?' the king asked immediately, black in the face. Even the court chamberlain, who was near the throne, had the same dark expression. 'Beware, if you're playing some sort of trick on me . . .'

"Buffello responded with a smile. He was thinking of the words his grandson had related to him the day before. 'It is the spirit of Christmas, Your Majesty. In other words, nothing. It is something you cannot see, touch, or taste. It is something that is born here.' He lightly tapped his chest with his forefinger. 'In our hearts. No alchemy could create a similar marvel.'

"'But then . . .' interjected the chamberlain. 'Snow, mistletoe, gifts, children's carols don't count for anything?'

"'Oh yes, they count,' replied the wizard. 'But only on the condition that you feel happy inside. If we are not good during the year, if we behave badly, a lack of Christmas spirit is not the reason. It all depends on us, even our own happiness. A heart of ice will surely not melt in the month of December.'

"The king remained absorbed in his thoughts for a few minutes. 'Sire, this man has swindled us,' whispered the chamberlain. 'I propose that we tie him to the torture wheel, then banish him from the kingdom.'

"'Oh, shut up, you viper!' the sovereign finally burst out. 'I believe you are precisely one of those with a heart of ice.' He lifted his scepter and rested it on the wizard's shoulder. 'Buffello, you have taught all of us a great lesson that we will never forget. In compensation, I command that you be given a thousand gold coins and a case of brand-new test tubes.'

"Buffello smiled contentedly, bowed to the king, and left the palace. Back in his laboratory, he found Buffetto. 'So, how did it go?' asked the boy. The wizard hugged him with all his might and kissed his brow. 'The king even gave me a reward! Naturally, we will split it.'

"Buffetto shook his head. 'No, Grampa, you keep it all for yourself. You deserve it. But remember: The spirit of Christmas either exists or doesn't exist. No one will ever be able to make it out of thin air. Never ever.'"

The

Snow

Comes

The fairy tale having ended, Grampa focused his gaze on Mark. "So, did you understand?"

The boy furrowed his brow. "Yes, I think so."

"That snowflake wasn't at all important. I mean, it was important to you because it represented Christmas. But the spirit of the holiday is in your soul, and no one can steal it from you."

"So, it doesn't matter if the snowflake turned to ice."

Grampa smiled. "Right. Just make sure that

the same thing doesn't happen to your heart. But I don't think you have to worry about that."

"But it was the first snowflake in December. For me, it was really important, and why I wanted to give it to the best person on earth." Mark pointed to his grandfather. "To you, I mean."

"Oh, thank you, but I don't think I am the best person of all. Everyone has their faults."

"Like what?" The boy was suddenly very interested.

The old man blushed. "Now is not the time to discuss them. Only remember that no one is born without flaws. Everyone has his or her own defects. It is important that he or she also have some virtues. That's all. People should be accepted as they are."

"Even the storekeeper, the doctor, and the philosophy professor?"

"Certainly."

All of a sudden, Mark's expression became sad. His eyebrows folded downward and his eyes dampened. Grampa Gus noticed immediately. "And now what's the matter?" he asked tenderly.

The boy took some time to reply. "I understood everything you just told me," he finally said. "But I was hoping to keep at least one snowflake, especially since I probably won't see any others."

"And who said so?"

Mark pointed out the window to the street, the lawn, and all the trees. "Look, the sky is clear. It probably won't snow until after Christmas. What kind of a holiday is it without snow?"

Grampa stood up and stared at the window. "Well, if that's all it is," he murmured. "You know, I have something to confess. I know just a little magic myself. Perhaps I am a distant relative of Buffello."

Mark stared at him in astonishment.

"Sometimes, in order to get your wish, all you need to do is concentrate and think about it very hard," said the old man. "C'mon, let's both give it a try."

"And what are we supposed to think about?"

asked the little boy. His grandfather's explanation had not been entirely clear.

"About the snow, of course!" exclaimed the old man. "And that Camolino decides to do his job!"

Mark bowed his head. "I pray to you, little angel," he began to say to himself. "C'mon, let it really come down. A beautiful white blanket, covering the houses and trees, so that children can play, sliding fast on their sleds and making big snowmen with carrot noses and button eyes."

The sky remained clear. There wasn't even the shadow of a snowflake.

"See," declared the boy, discouraged. "It doesn't work. It will never work."

"Are you absolutely sure about that?" Grampa asked him. "Look a little more closely, over there, among the clouds."

Mark got up and pressed his nose against the windowpane. Suddenly, he thought he saw, up high, a crooked halo, then a pair of short, short wings. He rubbed his eyes with the palm of his hand. It wasn't possible. The halo continued to shine in the sky, like a morning star.

"Grampa," he gasped, his heart filled to the brim with surprise. "It's Camolino!"

"Of course, it is he," replied Grampa Gus, putting his arm around his grandson. "He has finally decided to get to work."

"But how did you know? How did you reach him?"

"It was partly your doing. Children are close to angels, because they left them only a short time ago. And so are we old people, because it's not long until we join them again."

Among the clouds, there was a rapid beating of wings. A delicate, delicate wisp fell from the sky, then another, and then one after that. In a few minutes, the brown grass was covered with a sheet of bright white. And the tree branches changed from brown to marble white. The scene looked as if it had been drawn in chalk on a blackboard.

"Do you think it will keep snowing until tomorrow?" asked Mark, his voice full of hope.

"Yes, I do believe it will. Camolino is giving it his all." Grampa picked up his thriller. "Why don't you go outside and play?"

Mark didn't wait to hear him say it twice. Even the little voice spurred him along. "Go, go." He didn't even take off his pajamas. He ran to his bedroom, put on a sweater, then his windbreaker, and pulled on his boots.

Outside, the snowflakes danced a winter dance. Mark twirled around with them, gathering them with his fingers, letting them fall all over him, tasting them with the tip of his tongue. Their flavor was of magic and faraway lands. Millions of little white jewels, one for every good person on earth.

In the distance, he heard the echoing of bells. Christmas was arriving in great strides. Down the street, two other children were making snowballs and tossing them at each other. Mark joined them and shouted with joy.

The silence was growing, smothering the sounds and the hurried activities of the street: the silence of Christmas Eve.

Christmas

In the kitchen, Grampa looked upward. "Peace on earth," he murmured. He instinctively brought his hands together, palm against palm, in a gesture as old as the centuries but as modern as the millennium to come. "Peace on earth and good will to humankind."

High in the sky, from a tiny cloud, Camolino straightened his halo and winked.

And he continued to make the snow fall silently over the rooftops, over the trees, over the lawns and streets of Spring Valley, over the entire world.